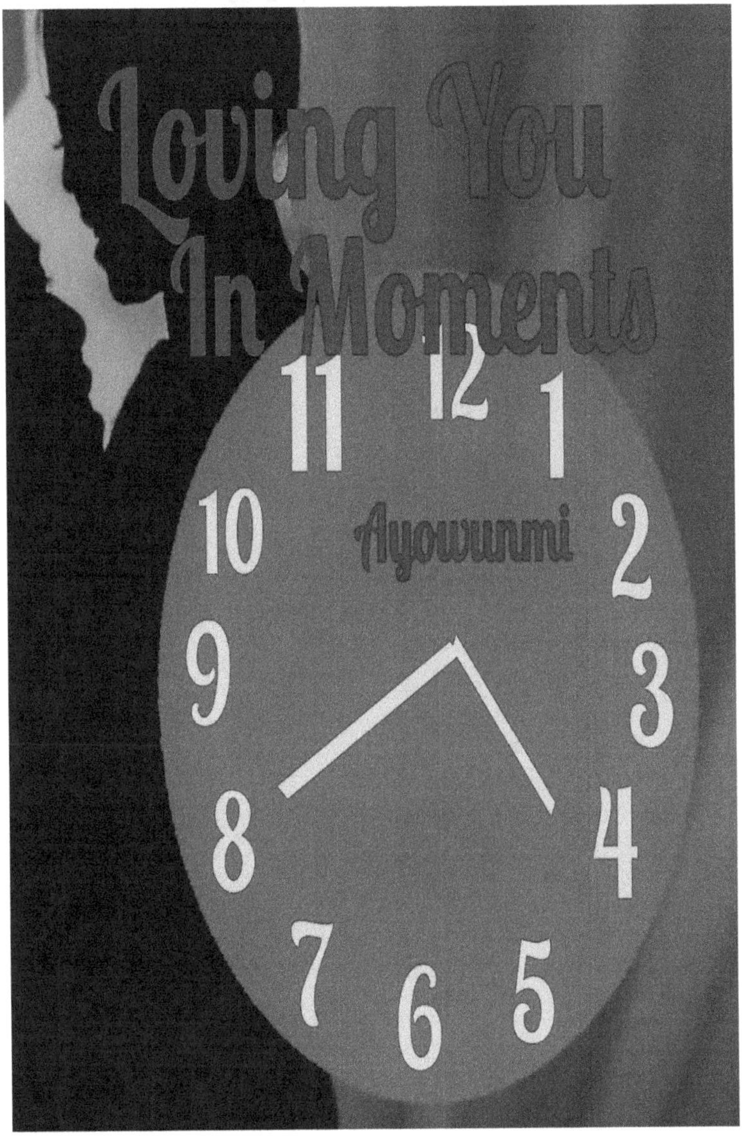
Loving You
In Moments
11 12 1
10 Ayowunmi 2
9 3
8 4
7 6 5

Divine Encounter Publishing

190 Shady Lane Drive Apt 124

Fort Worth, Texas 76112

Or

Email ihave1ngod@ gmail.com

Or call

817-363-6678

First print March 2022

Printed in Fort Worth, Texas

This book is dedicated to a man that God used to break the chains off of me …. I thank God for you.

CONTENT PAGE

PAGES   CHAPTERS

9 ARE YOU MY FRIEND OR MY ENEMY?

10 IT IS SPRINGTIME.

11 THE FUNNEL CAKE.

12 ROLLER COASTER

15 THOSE TREES

14 I WONDER WHAT I MEAN TO YOU

16 CHRISTMAS TREES

17 GOD SENT YOU TO BREAK MY CHAINS

19 A VOW TO A BOOK

22 I CELEBRATE YOUR LIFE

26 I GIVE YOU THE BEST OF ME

27 I HAD A DREAM

28 I MISS THE DAYS OF WHEN WE BEGAN

29 I POUR OUT MY HEART TO YOU

30 I SEE YOU CLEARLY

32 ICE CREAM

33 I WAITED BY THE PHONE

35 I SEE YOU IN MY DREAMS

37 BUT THE ROSE THAT YOU GAVE ME

39 I SIT AT MY DESK WANTING TO LOVE YOU

41 WHAT I WOULD SAY ON OUR WEDDING DAY

43 I'LL LIVE A DREAM

44 I'M BELIEVING IN THIS MOMENT

45 I'M LOVING YOU IN MOMENTS,

49 IN A TIME WHEN MY HEART WAS BROKEN

51 DO YOU REMEMBER

53 IN MY HEART THERE'S THE LOVE OF YOU

55 LET ME BAKE A CAKE FOR YOU

56 AROUND THE POND

59 THE FIRST TIME YOU SAID I LOVE YOU

61 LET ME EXSIST IN YOU

62 MY HEART CRIES

63 MY HEART SAYS BUT MY MIND SAYS

65 MY HEART WON'T STOP BEATING FOR YOU

67 THE WAY YOU LAY YOUR HEAD ON ME

68 ONLY GOD COULD WRITE OUR STORY

72 PSALM 91:4

73 INCASE I DIE

74 WHEN I LOOK INTO YOUR EYES

76 YOU ARE MY LIGHT

77 YOU WOKE ME UP

79 A BLESSING IN THE RAINING SEASON

81 MY VOWS

84 VISION OF WASHING THE CAR

86 BLOWING KISSES

87 WHEN ALL WE HAD WAS THAT MOMENT

89 PARALYZING KISSES

91 THE BALLERINA

93 THE RAIN POURED DOWN ON US LIKE A SHOWER

95 YOU AND I WILL ALWAYS BE

LOVING YOU IN MOMENTS

The word says that you can have hope , faith and love .

And the greatest of the three is love.

Without love, we have nothing.

Love is meant to be shared.

It is a feeling and an action.

It can build you up and destroy you.

Love should not hurt phsically or take away your peace.

ARE YOU MY FRIEND OR MY ENEMY?

ARE YOU MY FRIEND OR MY ENEMY?

ARE YOU THE ONE I CAN RUN TO?

THAT WILL HOLD ME AND WIPE MY TEARS AWAY.

OR ARE YOU THE ONE THAT I NEED TO GET AWAY FROM?

THE ONE THAT WILL HURT ME AND CAUSE ME PAIN.

ARE YOU MY FRIEND OR MY ENEMY?

DID GOD SEND YOU JUST FOR ME?

TO LOVE ME, COVER ME, TO BE THAT ONE?

ARE YOU MY FRIEND, THE ONE I CAN DEPEND UP ON?

THE ONE TO BE BY MYSIDE

LOVE ME IN SPITE OF?

THE ONE THAT I CAN TRUST?

OR ARE YOU MY ENEMY?

THE ONE WHO DOESN'T STAND CLOSE.

THE ONE WHO CAN'T LOVE UNLESS I CHANGE.

THE ONE WHERE THERE IS DOUBT.

ARE YOU MY FRIEND OR MY ENEMY?

WHICH ONE COULD IT BE?

IT IS SPRINGTIME.

IT IS SPRINGTIME.

AND I AM FEELING YOU.

HOW DOES IT FEEL TO BE CLOSE TO YOU?

FEEL YOUR HEARTBEAT

IT BLOWS MY MIND

COULD I BE IN LOVE WITH YOU?

HOW DOES IT FEEL TO BE TANGLED UP WITH YOU?

FEEL YOUR THOUGHTS

HOW YOU THINK.

I AM GOING CRAZY.

I NEED TO KNOW.

A MOMENT JUST TO SEE.

IT IS SPRINGTIME.

AND I AM FEELING YOU.

THE PUREST FORM OF YOU.

OH HOW I LONG FOR YOU.

AND RIGHT OR WRONG,

I FEEL THIS WAY.

I AM FEELING IN THIS SPACE.

IT'S SPRINGTIME.

THE FUNNEL CAKE.

THE FUNNEL CAKE.

THE SWEET TASTE.

WE SHARED PIECE BY PIECE.

WE SHARED BITE BY BITE.

NEVER HAVE I TASTED, A CAKE LIKE THIS.

IN MY MOUTH, I'M CAUGHT BY SURPRISE.

I SEE A GLIMPSE OF HAPPINESS.

A MOMENT< WHERE I FEEL BLESSED.

A SIMPLE THING,IT IS.

"YOU HAVE CINNAMON ON YOUR LIPS"

I SMILE AND LAUGH ,AS YOU WATCH ME.

I SAY TO MYSELF< "THIS IS AMAZING"

A FUNNEL CAKE FOR US

A SWEET, SWEET THING.

IN EVERY BITE LOVE IT MEANS.

ROLLER COASTER

A ROLLER COASTER,

SHOULD LOVE BE LIKE THIS?

A ROLLER COASTER RIDE.

SO FAST, SO WONDERFUL!

THE LOOK OF EXCITEMENT IN YOUR EYES.

SHOULD LOVE BE LIKE THIS?

HOLD ON TIGHT!

I SIT CLOSE TO YOU WITH EVERY TURN.

AND IT GETS FASTER, NEVER SLOWING DOWN.

I YELL REAL LOUD!

MY HEART BEATING FAST.

AND WE GO UP AND DOWN.

SHOULD LOVE BE LIKE THIS?

A ROLLER COASTER RIDE.

NO END TO THIS.

NO THOUGHT BUT FEELING.

IT'S LIKE I'M FLYING ON THE WIND.

WITH YOU WITH ME, I AM CONTENT.

SHOULD LOVE BE LIKE THIS?

A ROLLER COASTER RIDE.

THOSE TREES

I SAW THE TREES IN MY MIND.

IN A DREAM AS NIGHT PASSED BY.

I DIDN'T KNOW THE PLACE THAT THEY WOULD BE.

BUT I SAW THEM CLEARLY.

I WOKE UP.

AND I THOUGHT.

THOSE TREES, THOSE TREES.

THEY HAD MEANING.

EVERYWHERE I WENT I WOULD LOOK FOR THEM.

THEY HAD TO BE SOMEWHERE.

BUT THE TREES I DID NOT FIND.

UNTIL THAT DAY WE WENT FOR A RIDE.

I COULD NEVER IMAGINE THE TREES I WOULD SEE.

AS WE RODE DOWN THE HIGHWAY, TO THE RIGHT OF ME.

I SHOUTED!

THERE THEY ARE!

THOSE TREES, I SAW.

HOW BEAUTIFUL, THEY SEEM.

THOSE TREES FROM MY DREAM.

I WONDER WHAT I MEAN TO YOU

I WONDER WHAT I MEAN TO YOU

WHO I AM, IN YOUR HEART AND IN YOUR MIND?

YOU WANT TO KNOW HOW I FEEL

YOU ASK A QUESTION AND I GIVE YOU THE
ANSWER

YOU WANT TO KNOW

BUT YOU NEVER SAY.

YOU REFUSE TO SAY.

WHO AM I?

WHAT AM I?

I WONDER WHAT I MEAN TO YOU.

WHY CAN'T YOU JUST TELL ME!

YOU SAY WHEN YOU ARE READY.

THAT YOU CAN'T BE LIKE ME.

AND WEAR YOUR HEART ON A SLEEVE.

SO, YOUR HEART MUST STAY HIDDEN,

WHERE NO ONE CAN SEE.

I GET IT.

WHEN YOU ARE READY, YOU ARE READY.

WHEN YOU ARE NOT, YOU ARE NOT.

BUT WHEN WILL YOU SAY?

WHEN WILL YOU ASSURE ME?

SHOULD I JUST WAIT AND HOPE AND FEAR

CRY COUNTLESS TEARS.

I ASKED YOU WHAT I MEAN TO YOU.

WHY COME YOU JUST CAN'T SAY?

CHRISTMAS TREES

THERE I WAS WITH YOU, IN A FOREST OF
CHRISTMAS TREES.

OH! HOW THE TREES SHINED WITH LIGHTS.

EACH TREE DIFFERENT IN ITS OWN WAY

DIFFERENT COLORS,

GOLD, PINK, GREEN AND WHITE

NONE OF THEM WERE THE SAME

AND I YELLED,

"THIS ONE! THIS ONE!"

THE ONE WITH THE SNOW.

"YEAH. THAT'S THE ONE"

AND MY HEART JUMP WITH SO MUCH JOY

 I GOT EXCITED,

AS I SAW YOU PICK IT UP.

A FOREST OF CHRISTMAS TREES.

WHAT A PERFECT PLACE!

TO BE THERE YOU AND ME

I WAS SO AMAZED.

GOD SENT YOU TO BREAK MY CHAINS

THERE WERE CHAINS ON ME.

EACH ONE WITH A LOCK AND NO KEY.

I COULD MOVE WITHIN THE CHAINS.

BUT THERE WAS A LIMITED AMOUNT OF SPACE.

IN THESE CHAINS, I THOUGHT I WAS FREE.

BUT TO TELL THE TRUTH NOT FULLY.

GOD SAW MY DESPAIR.

HE SAW MY PAIN.

THAT'S WHEN HE SENT YOU

TO RELEASE MY CHAINS.

YOU WERE THE KEY FOR EVERY LOCK.

WITH YOU, ONE BY ONE WOULD OPEN UP.

GOD USED YOU TO BREAK MY CHAINS.

THERE WERE CHAINS ON ME.

HOLDING ME CAPTIVE AND KEEPING ME STILL

RELEASE ME IS WHAT I CRIED!

CHOKING ME CONSTANTLY.

I DIDN'T THINK THAT I WOULD SURVIVE.

GOD HE SAW.

YES, HE KNEW.

AND THAT'S WHY HE SENT YOU.

GOD USED YOU TO BREAK MY CHAINS.

USING YOUR STRENGTH AND YOUR LOVE IN
EVERY WAY.

A VOW TO A BOOK

GOD...GOD WROTE MY STORY.

HE WROTE THE CHAPTERS.

AND HE WROTE THEM, JUST FOR THIS DAY

HE CHANGED THE STORY THAT I HAD WROTE.

AND HE ERASED MY MISTAKES,

JUST FOR THIS MOMENT. FOR THIS VERY DAY.

THROUGHOUT MY LIFE, HE WROTE MANY BOOKS

 BUT TODAY, HE WRITES ONE THAT IS NEW.

GOD WRITES THE LAST ONE AND ONLY ONE WITH YOU.

THIS BOOK IS A NEW BEGINNING.

I PROMISE NOT TO BE AFRAID OF READING THE CHAPTERS

NO MATTER WHAT, I PROMISE TO KEEP READING.

I PROMISE TO LET GOD WRITE AND TO BE THE CO-WRITER,

GIVING THE WORDS WHEN NEEDED.

I PROMISE TO NEVER ASSUME WHAT THE CHAPTERS WILL BE.

NEVER TO GUESS AND LET IT BE A MYSTERY.

I PROMISE TO BE PRESENT IN THE CHAPTERS.

AND GIVE ALL, ALL I CAN TO OUR STORY.

I PROMISE TO PUT OUR BOOK HIGH ON A MANTLE ,BEFORE GOD THAT THE ENEMY CANNOT TOUCH,

EVEN ON HIS TIP TOES, THE ENEMY CAN NOT REACH

OUR BOOK WILL BE SO HIGH. LIKE THE STARS IN THE SKY.

WITH YOU THROUGH GOD, I PROMISE TO LIVE IN THE CHAPTERS EVERY DAY OF MY LIFE.

I PROMISE NOT TO READ WITHOUT YOU. NOT TO LIVE WITHOUT YOU

I MAKE A VOW.

NO ONE CAN TAKE YOUR PLACE

I WON"T READ WITH ANYONE ELSE.

ONLY WITH YOU THESE CHAPTERS , I WILL SHARE

MY BOOK CANNOT BE COMPLETED WITHOUT YOUR LOVE, SO I NEED YOUR CHAPTERS WRITTEN IN THERE

AND I PROMISE TO HOLD THEM CLOSE TO MY HEART AND MEND ANY PAGES.

I PROMISE TO FILL YOUR CHAPTERS WITH JOY AND LIFT YOU UP IN THEM.

I WILL NEVER THROW ANY PAGES AWAY.

THEY CAN NOT BE TORN.

NOR TARE THEM OUT OF THE BOOK.

WHATEVER WE GO THROUGH, WHATEVER STORM.

I WILL NOT LEAVE THIS BOOK BEHIND.

I WILL KEEP TURNING THE PAGES.

I WILL READ OUT LOUD

I WILL READ QUIETLY

I WILL BE FOCUSED

I WILL LOOK FOR THE MEANING IN EVERY
CHAPTER.

I WILL REMEMBER THAT THIS BOOK BELONGS TO
THE BOTH OF US.

IT IS US.

WITH YOU, I HAVE A BOOK

A SPECIAL BOOK OF LOVE

THAT I CANNOT AND WILL NOT PUT DOWN

BY THE GRACE OF GOD!

JULY 24TH 20018

I CELEBRATE YOUR LIFE

MMMM

MMM M MMMM

GOD MADE YOU WONDERFUL.

WITH A THOUGHT, HE MADE YOU!

AND YOU WERE SO SPECIAL.

WITH HIS HEART HE POURED IN TO YOU.

SO,

TODAY I CELEBRATE YOUR LIFE

IN EVERY WAY

 I CELEBRATE YOUR LIGHT

I CELEBRATE YOU

AND ALL THE THINGS YOU DO

I CELEBRATE YOU

JUST FOR BEING YOU

GOD MADE YOU PERFECTLY

WITH HIS HANDS FROM YOUR MOTHER'S WOMB

YOU WERE SOWN PIECE BY PIECE

HE TOOK TIME AND HE FORMED YOU

SO…..

TODAY I CELEBRATE YOUR LIFE

IN EVERY WAY

I CELEBRATE YOUR LIGHT

I CELEBRATE YOU

AND ALL THE THINGS YOU DO

I CELEBRATE YOU

JUST FOR BEING YOU

FOR BEING WHO YOU ARE

A SHINING STAR

I THANK GOD FOR YOU

TODAY I CELEBRATE YOUR LIFE

IN EVERY WAY

 I CELEBRATE YOUR LIGHT

I CELEBRATE YOU

AND ALL THE THINGS YOU DO

I CELEBRATE YOU

JUST FOR BEING YOU

I GIVE YOU THE BEST OF ME

I GIVE YOU MY HAND

PUT YOUR HAND IN MINE

AND I'LL NEVER LET IT GO

I'LL HOLD IT OH SO TIGHT

I'LL GIVE YOU MY EYES

AND YOU LOOK AT ME

AND I'LL NEVER TURN AWAY

I'LL ALWAYS SEE YOU

AND NO MATTER WHAT

 I'LL GIVE YOU THE BEST OF ME

FROM THE BEAT OF MY HEART

DOWN TO MY SOUL

I'LL GIVE YOU THE BEST OF ME

ALL I CAN GIVE

I'M YOURS TO HOLD

AS LONG AS I LIVE

HOLD ME CLOSE

I'LL GIVE YOU THE BEST OF ME

I'LL GIVE JOY WHEN YOU CRY

I'LL GIVE YOU THE SUNSHINE

I'LL ALWAYS TRY

I'LL GIVE YOU THE STARS

THE MOON AND MY WORLD

ALL THAT I AM

I'LL GIVE YOU MY MIND

GIVE ME YOUR THOUGHTS

AND I'LL NEVER STOP THINKING OF YOU

YOU'LL ALWAYS BE THERE

AND NO MATTER WHAT

I'LL GIVE YOU THE BEST OF ME

FROM THE BEAT OF MY HEART

DOWN TO MY SOUL

I'LL GIVE YOU THE BEST OF ME

ALL I CAN GIVE

I'M YOURS TO HOLD

AS LONG AS I LIVE

HOLD ME CLOSE

I'LL GIVE YOU THE BEST OF ME

I'LL GIVE JOY WHEN YOU CRY

I'LL GIVE YOU THE SUNSHINE

I'LL ALWAYS TRY

I'LL GIVE YOU THE STARS

THE MOON AND MY WORLD

ALL THAT I AM

I GIVE YOU THE BEST OF ME

I HAD A DREAM

I HAD A DREAM

A DREAM OF YOU.

STANDING IN FRONT OF ME IN A SUIT.

AND ALL I COULD WAS WALK TO YOU

STEP BY STEP.

LOOKING INTO YOUR EYES

COULDN'T WAIT TO GET TO YOU.

IT WAS A MUST.

COULD BARELY BREATHE INSIDE.

A DREAM COME TRUE.

I HAD A DREAM

A DREAM OF YOU.

WAITING PATIENTLY,

YOU WATCHED ME AS I WALKED DOWN,

YES, I SAW YOU WATCHING.

I KNEW I WOULD NOT TURN AROUND.

I HAD A DREAM

A DREAM OF YOU.

I MISS THE DAYS OF WHEN WE BEGAN

I MISS THE DAYS OF WHEN WE BEGAN

THE FIRST WORD OF US.

CURIOUS OF THE CHAPTER END

OF EACH MOMENT OF LOVE

I MISS THE DAYS OF OUR STORY.

THE FIRST LINE.

YOUR HELLO AND THEN MINE.

OH HOW IT WAS ALL SO NEW.

COULDN'T WAIT TO SEE WHAT WAS NEXT

I MISSED THE DAYS OF WHEN WE WERE.

OH! OUR FIRST DATE WAS THE BEST.

OF WHAT WE COULD HAVE BEEN.

EACH CHAPTER I WISH I COULD READ AGAIN.

I POUR OUT MY HEART TO YOU

I POUR OUT MY HEART TO YOU.

IN A THOUGHT,

IN A WHISPER,

IN A SONG.

I POUR OUT MY HEART TO YOU.

WITH MY SMILE,

A LOOK IN MY EYES,

JUST HOLDING YOUR ARMS.

I POUR OUT MY HEART TO YOU.

WHEN I SAY YOUR NAME,

WITH A HUG OR A KISS.

I POUR OUT MY HEART TO YOU.

I POUR OUT MY HEART TO YOU,

BY A TOUCH.

IT'S A MUST THAT I DO.

I POUR OUT MY HEART TO YOU.

IN SO MANY WAYS.

THAT I CAN'T THINK STRAIGHT.

I POUR OUT MY HEART TO YOU.

I SEE YOU CLEARLY

I SEE YOU.

I SEE YOU CLEARLY.

I SEE HOW YOU MOVE.

I SEE YOUR WAYS.

I SEE THE SMILE ON YOUR FACE.

I SEE YOU.

I SEE YOU CLEARLY.

I KNOW YOUR FEELINGS.

I KNOW YOUR MOODS.

I KNOW YOUR UPS AND YOUR DOWNS.

I KNOW HOW YOU ARE.

I KNOW THE GENTLE AND THE ROUGH PARTS.

I SEE YOU.

I SEE YOU CLEARLY.

I SEE YOUR LIGHT.

HOW BRIGHT YOU SHINE.

I SEE THE DARKNESS WHICH ONLY LASTS LITTLE
WHILE.

I SEE YOU.

YES,

A BEAUTIFUL YOU.

I SEE YOU AT YOUR BEST.

I SEE YOU CLEARLY.

31

ICE CREAM

I REMEMBER THAT DAY……

WE SAT ON A BENCH AND WE ATE ICE CREAM

I WATCHED YOU LICK ICE CREAM FROM THE STICK.

YOU WATCHED ME LICK MY LIPS.

THE SUN WAS SHINING SO BRIGHT,

AS MY ICE CREAM BEGAN TO MELT

IT WAS OKAY,

BECAUSE IN THAT SECOND, LOVE I FELT.

YOU FINISHED BEFORE I DID.

YEAH THAT'S RIGHT.

ME, I JUST TOOK MY TIME.

YOU WAITED AND SMILED.

I WAITED BY THE PHONE

I WAITED BY THE PHONE TO SEE IF YOU CALLED..

MINUTE BY MINUTE, I WAS CHECKING.

AND EVERY TIME I WAS DISAPPOINTED ,

IN YOU FOR NOT CALLING ME

IN ME, FOR EVEN ALLOWING MYSELF TO WAIT.

AND WHEN I COULD NOT WAIT ANY LONGER, I
FELL ASLEEP.

TO WAKE UP AND STILL NOT SEE A MISCALL

OH, EVERY ONE CALLED ME BUT IT DIDN'T
MATTER

I JUST WANTED ONE CALL FROM YOU.

I TOLD MYSELF THAT I WOULDN'T CALL YOU,

BUT I WANTED TO HEAR YOUR VOICE.

I MADE MYSELF LOOK WEAK.

FOR A PHONE CALL!

TO THINK THAT I DIDN'T EVEN MATTER;

THAT YOU WOULDN'T EVEN TAKE THE TIME.

I CHECKED MY MESSAGES.

I THOUGHT, IF AT LEAST YOU MESSAGE ME, I
WOULD STILL HAVE SOME PEACE.

I THOUGHT, IF YOU MESSAGED ME I WOULD HAVE
A LITTLE JOY,

BUT NOT A WORD

NOT A WORD!

AND THEN, I AM ANGRY

BUT WHY AM I ANGRY?

I HAD NO EXPECTATIONS.

YEAH, THAT'S THE LIE I TOLD.

I WANTED YOU.

MY HEART WANTED YOU.

MAYBE YOU THOUGHT ABOUT ME.

DID YOU?

I WONDER

BUT YOUR ACTIONS

THEY SHOWED ME.

I CALL YOU ONCE TWICE A DAY

AND I FEEL LIKE A BOTHER

I'M NOT IMPORTANT.

YOU CAN SEE MY NEEDS

AND YOU CAN'T SEE MY WANTS.

I'M NEEDY , A WHINER, EVEN A CRY BABY

ALL I WANTED WAS A PHONE CALL, A TEXT,
SOMETHING.

I SEE YOU IN MY DREAMS

I SEE YOU IN MY DREAMS.

I SEE YOU THERE WITH ME .

I SEE YOU.

I SEE YOU.

I SEE YOU SO CLEAR THAT I CAN'T DENY.

BEING RIGHT HERE FOR THE REST OF MY LIFE.

I SEE YOU, YOU GIVE ME JOY.

I SEE YOU STANDING TALL.

I SEE YOU IN MY DREAMS.

I SEE YOU THERE WITH ME.

I SEE YOU.

I SEE YOU.

IT SEEMS SO UNREAL.

LIKE A FANTASY.

DE JAVU.

LIKE A MEMORY.

I SEE YOU LIKE THE SUN.

I SEE YOU, SO WONDERFUL!

I SEE YOU IN MY DREAMS.

I SEE YOU THERE WITH ME.

I SEE YOU.

I SEE YOU.

BUT THE ROSE THAT YOU GAVE ME

THE ROSE THAT YOU GAVE ME

I LAUGH BECAUSE I NEVER THOUGHT THAT I
WOULD KEEP IT

I SAID TO MYSELF THAT IT WOULD ONLY LAST A
WEEK AND THEN DIE

EVERYDAY I PUT WATER IN THE VASE BUT I KEPT
THINKING THAT SOONER OR LATER IT WOULD DIE

AND WHEN I THINK ABOUT ALL THE OTHER ROSES
THAT I RECEIVED; YOUR ROSE IS THE ONLY ONE
THAT I WANTED TO KEEP LIVING

WHEN THE SEVENTH DAY CAME, I WAS AMAZED

TO SEE YOUR ROSE HAD BARELY CHANGE

I COULDN'T THROW IT AWAY

IT WAS STILL ALIVE AND I GUESS IT WAS GIVING
LIFE

TO WHAT YOU ASK?

THE LOVE INSIDE OF ME FOR YOU.

AND SEVEN DAYS BECAME A MONTH

AND THE ROSE PETAL WERE STILL RED

AND THE LEAVES WERE STILL GREEN

AND I REMINDED MYSELF TO PUT IN THE VASE.

YOUR ROSE, I WANTED TO KEEP

THEN A MONTH BECAME TWO

AS WE WERE CHANGING, I THOUGHT WHY KEEP
THIS ROSE?

BUT I HAD TO KEEP IT

IT IN ITSELF BECAME MOMENTS IN MY LIFE THAT
REMINDED ME OF YOU

IT'S PURPOSE WAS TO LIVE, TO CONTINUE

AND THOUGH IT MIGHT SOUND FUNNY AND A
LITTLE STRANGE

I WATCHED THE ROSE PETAL TURN BROWN AND
THE LEAVES CHANGE FROM GREEN

BUT STILL I WATERED

AND EVERYTIME I WAS IN SHOCKED

FOR IT KEPT DRINKING WATER.

IT DIDN'T STOP

I LOOKED AT IT BUT I DIDN'T WANT TO TOUCH IT

IN FEAR THAT A LEAF WOULD FALL

I THOUGHT HOW TO KEEP IT INTACT

WHAT COULD I DO?

THEN MORE MONTHS PASS AND THE ROSE WAS
JUST AS BEAUTIFUL AS WHEN YOU GAVE IT TO ME

DIFFERENT IN COLORS BUT EVERYTIME I SAW IT,
IT HAD MEANING

THE ROSE YOU GAVE ME WAS WORTH KEEPING

AND STILL I WATER IT AND WATCH IT.

I SIT AT MY DESK WANTING TO LOVE YOU

I SIT AT MY DESK WANTING TO LOVE YOU

YES, I HAVE THE DESIRE

BUT I AM NOT SURE IF I CAN

IF YOU WILL LET ME

YOU PUSH ME AWAY AND IT BREAKS PIECES OF MY HEART

I WANT TO FEEL YOU

FEEL YOUR LOVE

MAYBE TOUCH YOUR HEART

BUT YOU NEVER LET ME GET CLOSE ENOUGH

IT MESSES WITH MY MIND

WHY SHOULD I BOTHER?

I SIT AT MY DESK WANTING TO LOVE YOU

BUT IT'S SOMETHING THAT I CAN'T EVEN ATTEMPT

YOU WON'T LET ME

AND I AM MAD SOMETIMES AND I CRY SOMETIMES

CAUSE YOU DON'T UNDERSTAND

I WANT TO LOVE YOU

IT IS A NEED

HOW DARE YOU

YOU WON'T LET ME

WHAT I WOULD SAY ON OUR WEDDING DAY

I THOUGHT ABOUT WHAT I WOULD SAY TO YOU
ON OUR WEDDING DAY.

I IMAGINE JUST ME AND YOU,

AND A COUPLE OF WITNESSES,

I WALKED DOWN THE AISLE SO CAREFREE,

MY EYES ON YOU ALL THE WAY,

I GET MY PEN AND A PIECE OF PAPER

AND I THINK REAL HARD.

ALL THE WORDS I WANTED TO SAY,

ALL THE WORDS THAT I NEEDED TO SAY,

FIRST I'D TELL YOU I LOVE YOU

THROUGH GOOD TIMES AND BAD TIMES,

THROUGH SUNSHINE, STORMS AND RAIN.

THEN I'D MAKE A VOW,

TO LOVE YOU ALWAYS.

YEAH, THAT'S IT!

THEN I'D TELL YOU WHAT YOU MEAN TO ME.

MY ANCHOR ON TREACHEROUS SEAS

MY COMPASS…

I TURN AROUND!

ALL THOSE THINGS.

AND I'D SAY YOU'LL ALWAYS BE THOSE THINGS
TO ME.

THEN I'D SAY TO YOU,

THAT I GIVE MY HEART TO YOU

AND MAKE A CHOICE TO DO IT EVERY DAY.

I WILL PRAY FOR YOU AND LIFT YOU UP.

WHAT YOU GO THROUGH, I WILL GO THROUGH.

I WILL BELIEVE FOR YOU WHEN YOU CANNOT

I WILL NOT GIVE UP ON YOU OR US.

YES, I CAN SEE MYSELF,

STANDING WITH YOU.

I CAN SEE IT!

I LOOK DOWN AND

IN MY HAND A PIECE A PAPER.

I WROTE IT ALL DOWN,

JUST IN CASE

I FORGET THE WORDS.

THEN I OPEN UP MY HEART TO YOU.

I CRY WHILE SAYING EACH LINE, EACH VERSE.

EACH WORD I SAY IS A VOW.

NO HESITATION!

IN THAT MOMENT, THE MOMENT IT IS NOW.

I THOUGHT ABOUT WHAT I WOULD SAY TO YOU
ON OUR WEDDING DAY

I'LL LIVE A DREAM

43

I'LL LIVE A DREAM IN YOUR ARMS

I'LL LOSE MYSELF IN YOUR EYES

YOU'LL HOLD ME CLOSE AS CAN BE

AND I WILL CRY

TEARS OF ENDEARMENT

TEARS OF JOY

TEARS JUST BECAUSE

I'LL LIVE IN DREAM THAT NO OTHER CAN SHARE

FEELING YOU BREATHE

TOUCHING MY HAIR

WAKING UP TO YOUR LIGHT

IT OVERTAKES ME

BUT I CAN STAY THERE

I'LL LIVE IN A DREAM

IN MY OWN WORLD

AND ALL THAT I NEED IS YOU THERE

I'M BELIEVING IN THIS MOMENT

AND AS I LOOK UP INTO YOUR EYES

I AM BELIEVING IN THIS ONE MOMENT

I'M BELIEVING IN THIS MOMENT

THAT IF I SPEAK AND LOVE IS SPOKEN

THIS MOMENT WILL LAST THROUGHOUT OUR
LIVES

AND

WE'LL LOVE EACH OTHER TO THE ENDS OF TIME

LIVING IN A FANTASY

WE'LL BE THE ONES WHO LIVES A DREAM

I'M BELIEVING IN THIS MOMENT

THAT IF I SPEAK AND LOVE IS SPOKEN

WE'LL BE A WITNESS TO A MIRACLE

AND PROVE THAT NOTHING'S IMPOSSIBLE

LIVING IN A FANTASY

WE'LL BE THE ONES WHO LIVE A DREAM

I'M LOVING YOU IN MOMENTS,

I'M LOVING YOU IN MOMENTS,

AS THE DAYS GO BY.

I'M LOVING YOU IN MOMENTS,

THROUGHOUT, OUT TIME.

I'M LOVING YOU IN MOMENTS,

AS THE SECONDS PASS.

I'M LOVING YOU IN MOMENTS.

MAY THEY LAST?

I'M LOVING YOU IN MOMENTS,

THE GOOD AND THE BAD.

I'M LOVING YOU IN MOMENTS.

AS EACH MOMENT MIGHT COME,

I'M LOVING YOU.

MINUTE BY MINUTE,

HOUR BY HOUR,

I'M LOVING YOU.

I'M LIVING YOU IN MOMENTS,

WHEN YOUR ARMS ARE AROUND ME.

I'M LOVING YOU IN MOMENTS, WHEN I CAN HEAR
YOU BREATHE.

I'M LOVING YOU IN MOMENTS,

WHEN THERE'S NO SOUND.

I'M LOVING YOU IN MOMENTS, WHEN THE SUN'S
SHINING DOWN

I'M LOVING YOU IN MOMENTS,

THE GOOD AND THE BAD.

AS EACH MOMENT MIGHT COME,

I'M LOVING YOU.

MINUTE BY MINUTE,

HOUR BY HOUR

I'M LOVING YOU.

I'M LOVING YOU IN MOMENTS, WHEN I CAN FEEL
THE WIND.

I'M LOVING YOU IN MOMENTS, WHEN YOU HOLD
MY HAND.

I'M LOVING YOU IN MOMENTS,

THE GOOD AND THE BAD.

AS EACH MOMENT MIGHT COME,

I'M LOVING YOU.

MINUTE BY MINUTE,

HOUR BY HOUR,

I'M LOVING YOU.

I'M LOVING YOU IN MOMENT,

AS THE SEASON CHANGE.

IN THE FALL, SUMMER AND WINTER

AND IN THE SPRING.

I'M LOVING YOU IN THE RAIN.

I'M LOVING YOU IN MOMENTS,

THE GOOD AND THE BAD.

AS EACH MOMENT MIGHT COME,

I'M LOVING YOU.

MINUTE BY MINUTE,

HOUR BY HOUR

I'M LOVING YOU.

I'M LOVING YOU IN MOMENTS,

AS THE WORLD IT TURNS.

I'M LOVING YOU IN MOMENTS, AS THE STARS,
THEY SHINE

WHEN I LOOK INTO YOUR EYES.

I'M LOVING YOU IN MOMENTS,

THE GOOD AND THE BAD.

AS EACH MOMENT MIGHT COME,

I'M LOVING YOU.

MINUTE BY MINUTE,

HOUR BY HOUR

I'M LOVING YOU.

IN A TIME WHEN MY HEART WAS BROKEN

IN A TIME WHEN MY HEART WAS BROKEN

 A PRAYER TO GOD I SPOKE AND

AND SUDDENLY YOU WERE THERE

I CAN'T BELIEVE YOU ARE HERE

YOU ARE HERE

AND THE WORDS CAME POURING OUT

AND EVERY WORD HE HEARD FROM MY MOUTH

GOD MEND THESE BROKEN PIECES

MAKE MY HEART WHOLE AGAIN

IN MY HANDS, I GIVE THEM TO YOU

AND THEN

IN A TIME WHEN MY HEART WAS BROKEN

I HAD EVERYTHING

AND THEN I HAD NOTHING

WHAT WAS I TO DO?

WHAT COULD BE DONE, ONLY GOD KNEW?

HE HEARD MY PRAYER THIS I KNOW

FOR YOU WERE THERE, MY HOPE

IN A TIME WHEN MY HEART WAS BROKEN

I COULD NOT FEEL

MY HEART SHATTERED IN PIECES

THEY LAID ON THE GROUND

AND I SCREAMED AND I SCREAMED

AND GOD HEARD THE SOUND

FOR I SAW YOU, WHEN I LOOKED AROUND

IN A TIME WHEN MY HEART WAS BROKEN

A PRAYER TO GOD I SPOKE AND

AND SUDDENLY YOU WERE THERE

I CAN'T BELIEVE YOU ARE HERE

YOU ARE HERE

DO YOU REMEMBER

DO YOU REMEMBER WATCHING THE TIMEKEEPERS WIFE, THE MOVIE?

YOU SAT ON THE COUCH AND WATCHED IT WITH ME.

WE LAUGHED ABOUT IT.

I THINK THAT IT WAS IN THAT MOMENT, I UNDERSTOOD…

I WAS JUST LIKE THE TIMEKEEPERS WIFE.

I WAS LOVING YOU IN MOMENTS.

GOD WAS MAKING ME, NO FORCING ME TO DEAL WITH ISSUES IN MY LIFE.

AND AS I DEALT WITH THOSE ISSUES, YOU WERE PRESENT IN MINUTES AND HOURS

THE ONE THING THAT I WAS SURE OF IS THAT I COULD LOVE YOU AS TIME PASSED BY.

I COULD TRUST THAT.

WHEN YOU WERE IN THE MOMENT, I COULD FEEL YOUR THOUGHTS AND YOUR HEART

AND I WAS WITH YOU IN THE MOMENT.

AND THERE WAS LOVE

BUT JUST LIKE THE WIFE IN THE MOVIE, I HAD TO DEAL WITH THE MOMENTS THAT YOU WASN'T THERE.

I WAS MAD AT FIRST BUT I REALIZED YOU WERE JUST LIKE THE HUSBAND YOU HAD NO CHOICE.

SOME MOMENTS, YOU WERE NOT GOING TO BE IN
BUT EVEN STILL I LOVED YOU ANYWAY.

IN MY HEART THERE'S THE LOVE OF YOU

IN MY HEART THERE IS A LOVE I CAN'T EXPLAIN

THERE'S A LOVE THAT WILL NEVER CHANGE

IN MY HEART IT'S YOU, THE LOVE OF YOU

IT'S YOU

IN MY HEART THERE'S A LOVE THAT WILL NEVER
GO

 IN MY HEART A LOVE THAT WILL BE WHEN I
GROW OLD

IN MY HEART A LOVE THAT WILL FOLLOW ME

A LOVE THAT WILL ALWAYS BE

IN MY HEART, IT'S YOU, THE LOVE OF YOU

IN MY HEART THERE'S A LOVE IN ME THAT MAKES
ME SMILE

LIKE THE WIND IT CARRIES ME AWAY

LIKE THE SUN SHINING DOWN UPON MY FACE

IN MY HEART IT'S YOU, THE LOVE OF YOU

IN MY HEART THERE'S A LOVE THAT MAKES ME
SING, A MELODY

A LOVE THAT BURIED OH SO DEEP INSIDE OF ME

A LOVE THAT FLOWS THROUGH ME

A LOVE THAT GOES THROUGH ME

IN MY HEART IT'S YOU THE LOVE OF YOU

IN MY HEART IT'S THE LOVE OF YOU

IN MY HEART THERE'S A LOVE THAT'S ALWAYS
AROUND

IT WILL BE WITH ME ALL OF MY LIFE

IN MY HEART I'M PARALYZED WHEN YOU KISS ME

I CAN'T MOVE WHEN YOU KISS ME

IT PUTS ME A DAZE

YOUR KISS HAS ME MEMORIZED

AND ALL I CAN DO IS BE STILL

LET ME BAKE A CAKE FOR YOU

YOU TOLD ME A STORY ABOUT YOUR
GRANDMOTHER.

YOU SAID THAT SHE ALWAYS MADE A CAKE .AND
SO THAT YOU WOULDN'T GET UPSET, SHE MADE
YOUR OWN SPECIAL CAKE.

YOU'D WAKE UP AND SMELL IT.

THEN, YOU WOULD COME INTO THE KITCHEN AND
EAT A SLICE.

HEARING THAT ALWAYS MADE ME WANT TO
BAKE YOU A CAKE.

I WANTED TO SEE JOY IN YOUR EYES

THE INNOCENCE OF A CHILD

IT MUST HAVE BEEN A WONDERFUL THING

TO SEE YOU THAT HAPPY

I WANTED TO SEE JOY IN YOUR EYES

PURE AND KIND

SOFT AND MOIST, EVERY TASTE OF IT

AND OH! SO SWEET.

LET ME BAKE A CAKE FOR YOU

SO YOU CAN HAVE THAT FEELING.

EATING EVER PIECE

NOT LEAVING A CRUMB

YOU KNEW IT WAS MADE WITH SO MUCH LOVE

YOU GRANDMA WAS HAPPY TO SEE YOU SMILE

IT DID HER GOOD JUST TO SEE

LET ME BAKE A CAKE FOR YOU

SO I CAN EXPERIENCE WHAT YOUR GRANDMA DID

AROUND THE POND

WE WALKED AROUND THE POND

AS WE WALKED AROUND THE POND.

I NOTICED TURTLES IN THE WATER.

THERE'S ONE!

THERE'S ONE!

I SHOUTED.

CAN YOU SEE THE TURTLES?

CATCH ME ONE.

AND YOU LAUGHED.

LOOK THERE'S ONE ON A ROCK.

THERE'S ONE WITH ITS HEAD UP.

I PUSHED YOU.

AND SAID, "GO INTO THE WATER AND GET ME ONE."

AND YOU LAUGHED AND SAID NO.

THEN

YOU SAID," THEY ARE UNDER THE WATER"

WHERE? "I ASKED.

 I SAID, "I DON'T SEE THEM"

AND YOU POINTED AT THEM.

I SMILED AT YOU.

AND YOU LAUGHED AT ME

WE WALKED THE POND AND SAW TURTLES

THE FIRST TIME YOU SAID I LOVE YOU

THE FIRST TIME YOU SAID I LOVE YOU,

IT WAS NIGHTTIME AND VERY QUIET.

AND IN A WHISPER, I HEARD I LOVE YOU.

I THOUGHT, DID YOU MEANT TO SAY IT?

WERE YOU ASLEEP?

MY EYES WERE OPEN, BUT WAS I DREAMING?

I REMEMBER SMILING.

I REMEMBER THINKING...

IN THIS MOMENT, I COULD KISS YOU.

MAKE LOVE TO YOU.

BUT I WASN'T SURE.

I WASN'T SURE IF YOU MEANT TO SAY IT.

OR IF I WAS MEANT TO HEAR IT.

I WANTED YOU TO LOOK AT ME.

I WANTED TO SEE YOUR LIPS MOVE.

YOU SAID IT AGAIN.

I HEARD YOU THIS TIME.

THE WORDS I LOVE.

WHAT A WONDERFUL SOUND

THE SOUND OF YOUR VOICE.

THE SOUND OF THOSE THREE WORDS.

MY HEART ALMOST STOPPED.

I SMILED UNTIL I FELL ASLEEP.

WITH YOU, NEXT TO ME.

LET ME EXIST IN YOU

LET ME EXIST IN YOU, JUST THE WAY I AM.

LET ME BE APART YOU.

SAY YES, SO THAT I CAN.

LET ME BE IN YOU.

FEEL YOU AND KNOW YOU.

LET ME EXIST IN YOU.

LET ME TOUCH YOU FROM YOUR SOUL.

GO WHERE OTHERS DID NOT WANT TO GO.

LET ME HEAR YOUR HEARTBEAT.

LIKE A SONG.

GO DEEP WITH YOU.

LIKE THE OCEAN.

LET ME EXIST IN YOU.

KNOW EVERY PART OF YOU.

FROM YOUR VERY CORE.

LET ME EXIST IN YOU.

LET ME IF YOU CAN.

LET ME EXIST IN YOU.

KNOW YOU FROM WITHIN.

MY HEART CRIES

MY HEART CRIES.

LISTENING TO YOU LIKE A SAD, SAD SONG.

TEARS THEY FALL.

I CAN FEEL YOUR SOUL.

MY HEART CRIES.

I CAN FEEL YOU, YOUR VERY EXISTENCE.

I WISH I COULD EXIST IN YOU.

BUT THERE IS RESISTANCE.

MY HEART CRIES AND YOU ARE NOT AWARE.

THERE ARE MOMENTS THAT I WONDER IF YOU CARE.

AND OH THAT PAINS ME SO.

TO WONDER.

TO NEVER KNOW.

MY HEART CRIES.

I FEEL YOUR THOUGHTS.

THE PURIST FORM OF THEM.

AND I CAN'T HELP THE WAY THAT I FEEL.

MY HEART CRIES.

MY HEART SAYS BUT MY MIND SAYS

MY HEART SAYS TO LOVE YOU BUT MY MIND
SAYS TO BEWARE.

I SEE YOU HERE BUT SOMETIMES YOU ARE NOT
THERE.

YOU INTRIGUE ME.

YOU MAKE ME WANT MORE.

BUT MY MIND SAYS NO.

MY HEARTS WANTS TO GIVE YOU ALL WITHOUT A
QUESTION.

BUT MY MIND SAYS I NEED DIRECTION.

YOU MESS WITH MY HEART AND CONFUSE MY
MIND.

MY HEART IS SURE, BUT MY MIND HAS DOUBT.

MY HEART SAYS TO LOVE YOU BUT MY MIND
STAYS TO STOP.

CAUSE LOVING YOU CAN COST.

COST PIECES OF ME.

BUT I GIVE YOU MYSELF WILLING.

YOU COULD DESTROY,

EVERY PART OF ME.

BUT MY HEART WOULD TAKE THE CHANCE.

MY MIND SAYS BE CAREFUL.

BUT HOW CAN I?

WHEN MY HEARTS FEELS WHAT IT FEELS INSIDE.

MY HEART WON'T STOP BEATING FOR YOU

MY HEART WON'T STOP BEATING FOR YOU

IT WON'T STOP CALLING YOUR NAME

NO MATTER WHAT WE GO THROUGH

IT BEATS JUST THE SAME

IT BEATS FOR YOU

SOMETIMES WE FUSS AND WE FIGHT AND YOU
MAKE ME CRY

SOMETIMES I MAKE YOU ANGRY AND MAD AND
THINGS ARE NOT RIGHT

AND SOMETIMES YOU YELL AND SOMETIMES I
SCREAM

AND SOMETIMES YOU WON'T LOOK AT ME

BUT MY HEART WON'T STOP BEATING FOR YOU

IT WON'T STOP CALLING YOUR NAME

NO MATTER WHAT WE GO THROUGH

IT STILL BEATS JUST THE SAME

IT BEAT FOR YOU

SOMETIMES I WANNA GIVE UP AND YOU DON'T
WANNA TRY

IN MY MIND I'VE HAD ENOUGH AND YOU TELL ME
GOODBYE

AND SOMETIMES I CAN'T HEAR YOU

YOU TURN YOUR BACK ON ME

SOMETIMES I CAN'T BE NEAR YOU

IT'S HARD TO SEE

BUT MY HEART WON'T STOP BEATING FOR YOU

IT CAN'T STOP CALLING YOUR NAME

NO MATTER WHAT WE GO THROUGH

MY HEART BEATS JUST THE SAME

IT BEATS FOR YOU

THE WAY YOU LAY YOUR HEAD ON ME

THE WAY YOU LAY YOUR HEAD ON ME,

HOW ENDEARING IT IS.

I TAKE MY HAND AND TOUCH YOUR FACE.

THE WAY YOU LAY YOUR HEAD ON ME,

SO TENDER AND KIND.

HUMBLING YOURSELF TO THAT VERY SPOT ON ME,

AS IF YOU FIND COMFORT ON ME.

IN SUCH A GENTLE WAY.

THE WAY YOU LAY YOUR HEAD ON ME,

NO ONE HAS EVER DONE.

YOUR OWN SPECIAL PLACE.

MADE JUST FOR YOU, ONLY YOU.

THERE, THAT'S WHERE YOU GIVE ME YOUR HEART.

AND I AM AT PEACE.

THE WAY YOU LAY YOUR HEAD ON ME,

FEELING YOU SO CLOSE.

I CAN FEEL WHAT YOU ARE THINKING

I CAN YOUR SOUL.

ONLY GOD COULD WRITE OUR STORY

ON-LY GOD

ON-LY GOD

ONLY GOD COULD WRITE THIS STORY NO ONE
ELSE IT COULD BE

HE TOOK HIS PEN AND HE WROTE IT ENDLESSLY

HE TOOK A PRAYER AND MADE IT COME TRUE

I TURN AROUND AND THERE WAS YOU

PAGE FOR PAGE

DAY AFTER DAY

HE WROTE THE WORDS EVERY PAGE

WRITTEN IN LOVE TO LAST ALWAYS

WRITTEN SO PERFECTLY

THE LOVE OF YOU AND ME

WRITTEN SO PERFECTLY

IT WAS LIKE A DREAM

ON-LY GOD

ON-LY GOD

ONLY GOD COULD WRITE THIS STORY THERE'S NO
ONE ELSE

HE HAD TO WRITE IT ALL BY HIMSELF

HE DREW THE MOMENTS ONE BY ONE

 EVERY MOMENT HE DREW OF US

HE WROTE THE WORDS EVERY PAGE

WRITTEN IN LOVE TO LAST ALWAYS

WRITTEN SO PERFECTLY

THE LOVE OF YOU AND ME

WRITTEN SO PERFECTLY

IT WAS LIKE A DREAM

LIKE A FANTASY

HE DREW THE SUNSHINE

AND THE STORMS HE DREW

BUT IN EVERY LINE

AND WE MADE IT THROUGH

HE WROTE THE WORDS EVERY PAGE

WRITTEN IN LOVE TO LAST ALWAYS

WRITTEN SO PERFECTLY

THE LOVE OF YOU AND ME

WRITTEN SO PERFECTLY

IT WAS LIKE A DREAM

LIKE A FANTASY

ON-LY GOD

ONLY GOD

ONLY GOD COULD WRITE A STORY OF THIS LOVE

HE BINDED THE PAGES, NO ONE COULD TEAR
APART

HE SEWED THEM WITH THE BEATS OF OUR
HEARTS

HE WROTE THE WORDS EVERY PAGE

WRITTEN IN LOVE TO LAST ALWAYS

WRITTEN SO PERFECTLY

THE LOVE OF YOU AND ME

WRITTEN SO PERFECTLY

IT WAS LIKE A DREAM

LIKE A FANTASY

TO STAND THE TEST OF TIME

HE WROTE EVERY LINE

PAGE AFTER PAGE

WRITTEN SO PERFECTLY

THE LOVE OF YOU AND ME

WRITTEN SO PERFECTLY

IT WAS LIKE A DREAM

LIKE A FANTASY

PSALM 91:4

HE SHALL COVER THEE WITH HIS FEATHERS, AND
UNDER HIS WINGS SHALT THOU TRUST: HIS TRUTH
SHALL BE THY SHIELD AND BUCKLER.

THIS WAS THE VERSE THAT I FOUND YOU IN.

I REMEMBER SITTING IN CHURCH AND OUR
READING WAS PSALMS 91.

AS WE BEGAN TO READ THIS, I DIDN'T THINK
MUCH ABOUT IT.

THEN WE READ VERSE 4

GOD REVEALED TO ME THAT HE SENT YOU TO ME
TO COVER ME

HE DIDN'T SAY HOW LONG

BUT HE SAID I COULD TRUST THE WINGS; I COULD
TRUST YOU

AND THERE I COULD FIND GOD'S TRUTH AND HE
WOULD PROTECT ME AND SHIELD ME.

INCASE I DIE

73

I DIDN'T KNOW IF I WOULD LEAVE YOU A LETTER IF I DIED, BUT MY HEART DID.

I LOVE YOU. YOU WERE MY TEST, MY NEW BEGINNING.

GOD USED YOU TO BREAK MY CHAINS AND SET ME FREE.

I WISH I COULD PINCH THOSE FAT CHICKS AND THEN KISS THEM. ANY WAY JUST KNOW THAT YOU ARE SPECIAL AND MUCH LOVED.

NO MATTER WHAT IT LOOKED LIKE, YOU WERE EVERYTHING TO ME.

I WISH THAT WE COULD HAVE HAD MORE TIME.

KNOW THAT JUST BECAUSE I AM NOT THERE DOES NOT MEAN I HAVE STOPPED LOVING YOU.

IF MY SPIRIT CARRIED ON AND I YET LIVE, KNOW THAT MY LOVE FOR YOU STILL LIVES.

LOVE CAN LAST A LIFETIME.

6/22/2020

1:11 PM

WHEN I LOOK INTO YOUR EYES

WHEN I LOOK INTO YOUR EYES,

I GET THE STRANGEST FEELING THAT I HAVE SEEN
YOU ONCE BEFORE.

MAYBE I'M DREAMING.

WHEN I LOOK INTO YOUR EYES,

I CANNOT EXPLAIN.

I'VE SEEN YOU.

I HAVE SEEN YOU FACE.

WHEN I LOOK INTO YOUR EYES,

I HAVE NO DOUBT THAT I'VE SEEN YOU.

MAYBE SOMEWHERE, IN ANOTHER PLACE.

MAYBE SOMEWHERE, I CANNOT TRACE.

WHEN I LOOK INTO YOUR EYES, I DON'T KNOW

BUT THEM, I HAVE SEEN.

MAYBE FROM YEARS AGO.

WHEN I LOOK INTO EYES,

I'VE SEEN YOU BEFORE.

I COULD SWEAR,

WHEREVER YOU MIGHT HAVE BEEN, I WAS THERE.

WHEN I LOOK INTO YOUR EYES,

I HAVE SEEN YOU.

MAYBE IN ANOTHER TIME.

MAYBE JUST PASSING THROUGH.

WHEN I LOOK INTO YOUR EYES,

 I AM SO SURE,

I HAVE SEEN YOU

YOU ARE MY LIGHT

I SEE MYSELF OLD WITH YOU.

I WAKE UP TO YOUR EYES

WITH A SMILE ON YOUR FACE,

YOU SIT BY MYSIDE nd in your eyes I gaze.

IN YOUR HANDS IS A GIFT,

A SMALL RED BOX.

YOU OPEN IT

AND A CHAIN YOU PULL OUT.

YOU TAKE IT AND GENTLY PUT IT AROUND MY
NECK.

AND YOU SAY "THIS IS SO YOU NEVER FORGET"

AT THE END OF THE CHAIN IS A LIGHT HOUSE

AND YOU SAY "YOU ARE MY LIGHT"

AND YOU HOLD ME TIGHT.

THEN, YOU KISS ME

AND I AM SO HAPPY.

YOU WOKE ME UP

I HAD A DREAM THAT YOU WOKE ME UP.

THERE I WAS IN A HOUSE, OUR HOUSE

AND I AM AWAKEN BY THE SOUND.

I EAR THE LAWN MOWER.

YOU GOT UP EARLY TO DO WHAT MEN DO.

YOU WASN'T TRYING TO DISTURB ME

I JUST WOKE UP AS YOU PUSHED THE LAWN
MOWER THROUGH.

I'M THINKING,

WHY IS HE UP SO EARLY?

I'M THINKING,

IT'S EIGHT O'CLOCK ON SATURDAY

I LOOKD OUT OF THE WINDOW TO SEE IF I COULD
SEE YOU

AND WHEN I GET A GLIMPSE OF YOU,

I SHAKE MY HEAD AND SMILE

AND I SAY TO MYSELF

I AM GOING BACK TO BED AND SLEEP FOR
AWHILE.

BUT OH THAT SOUND.

 THE LAWN MOWER KEEPS ME A WAKE.

I HAVE TAKEN ALL THAT I COULD TAKE

SO, I GET UP

AND FIX YOU A POT OF RICE

AND THINK, TO BE WAKEN UP BY YOU, FEELS
PRETTY NICE.

A BLESSING IN THE RAINING SEASON

I DON'T EVER WANT YOU TO THINK THAT OUR MOMENTS TOGETHER WAS A MISTAKE.

I KNOW THAT THEY WERE NOT.

YOU WERE A BLESSING TO ME.

WHEN I NEEDED A BLESSING, GOD SENT YOU.

IT WAS RAINING SO HARD IN MY LIFE.

THE RAIN COVERED ME

AND I WAS DROWNING IN MY MISTAKES, MY REGRETS

I HAD LOST EVERYTHING .

I WAS SOAKED IN LOST LOVE

AND THE IMAGE OF MYSELF.

AND IT WOULDN'T STOP!

THE RAIN WOULD NOT STOP!

IT WAS THE RAINING SEASON.

I STOOD OUT IN THE RAIN BECAUSE THERE WAS NO WHERE TO GO.

 THE ONLY PLACE TO GO WAS WHERE GOD STOOD.

AND EVEN WHEN I WAS STANDING IN THERE , THE RAIN POURED DOWN ON ME.

IT WAS STILL RAINING.

SO IN THE MIDST OF THE RAIN, I ASK HIM FOR ONE THING.

I ASKED HIM FOR A COVERING

AND IN MY RAINING SEASON GOD SENT YOU

AND I WAS BLESSED!

NO YOU DIDN'T COME AS SUNSHINE

AND THE RAIN DIDN'T STOP.

BUT WHEN I SAW YOU, I SAW A COVERING

 I SAW A PLACE THAT I COULD GO TO GET OUT OF THE RAIN

A PLACE TO BE WARM AND TO BE AT PEACE

YOU SEE YOU WERE MY BLESSING

MY VOWS

TODAY GOD HAS PREPARED ME TO BE YOUR
WIFEAND TODAY GOD GAS FORFILLED A PROMISE.

HE HAS CREATED IN ME A NEW CREATURE,
WASHING ME IN HIS BLOOD AND HE HAS GIVEN
ME A NEW HEART AND WITH THIS HEART I VOW
TO LOVE YOU UNCONDITIONALLY

JUST AS GOD HAS LOVED ME, I WILL LOVE YOU.

I WILL LOVE YOU FOR ALL OF MY DAYS

AND I PRAISE GOD NOW

AS I STAND BEFORE YOU, KNOWING THAT I AM
MADE FOR ONLY YOU AND I AM MEANT FOR ONLY
YOU

ALWAYS BELONGING TO GOD

I MAKE A VOW TO PRAY FOR YOU,

PRAY WITH YOU,

CRY WITH YOU

CRY FOR YOU

NEVER TARING YOU DOWN

MY HOPE IS TO BUILD YOU UP

AND ALWAYS CELEBRATING WHAT WE HAVE

AS I LOOK AT YOU, I LOOK AT MY PROMISE

IT COULD HAVE BEEN ANYONE BUT I AM SO GLAD
THAT IT'S YOU.

I PROMISE TO NEVER LOOSE SIGHT OF WHO YOU
ARE

WHAT YOU ARE

OR WHAT YOU MEAN TO ME

I WILL ALWAYS TRY, NEVER GIVING UP ON US

BELIEVING IN GOD AND US

AND I WILL BE BY YOURSIDE WHEN THE RAIN IS
COMING DOWN

I WILL STAND IN FAITH WITH YOU

EVEN WHEN I CAN NOT SEE, I WILL GO THROUGH
THE STORMS HOLDING ON TO YOU AND TO GOD'S
UNCHANGING HAND

AND AS I HOLD ON TO YOUR HANDS I WILL NOT
LET GO.

NEVER LETTING GO, NEVER TURNING AWAY FROM
GOD OR YOU

I MAKE A VOW TO GIVE YOU MY BEST

TO GIVE YOU MY ALL

PRAISING GOD FOR OUR MOMENTS TOGETHER

IN EVERY MOMENT, THE GOOD AND THE BAD.

AND OH YES THE UGLY.

IN SICKNESS AND IN HEALTH

I'LL BE THERE WITH YOU

NEVER CHANGING MY MIND

NO ONE WILL COME BETWEEN US

NOTHING WILL STAND AGAINST US

NO WEAPON WILL BE FORMED

YOU WILL HAVE MY TRUST, FOR ALL THE DAYS
OF MY LIFE

I MAKE THIS VOW THIS OATH; THIS PROMISE TO
BE THE WIFE THAT GOD HAS PREPARED ME TO BE
FOR YOU.

DECEMBER 21,2017

VISION OF WASHING THE CAR

YOU WERE OUTSIDE TRYING TO WASH THE CARS

AND I WAS OUTSIDE WITH YOU

YOU HAD THE WATER HOSE IN YOUR HAND AND
YOU WERE ABOUT TO WET THE CAR

WHEN I OPENED THE PASSENGER BACK DOOR

WHAT ARE YOU DOING?"' YOU ASKED.

I SAID," I AM TRYING TO CLEAN THE CAR OUT

YOU TOLD ME TO MOVE.

AND I TOLD YOU NO.

"I AM CLEANING THE CAR

YOU SAID," HURRY UP."

AND I SAID SOMETHING LIKE

"YOU'RE GONNA HAVE TO WAIT."

WELL, YOU DIDN'T WAIT.

YOU BEGAN TO SPRAY THE CAR WITH WATER

"STOP!" I YELLED, WHILE I WAS LAUGHING,"
YOU'RE GONNA GET ME WET!"

"WELL HURRY UP THEN", YOU SAID

THEN I STARTED HUMMING

AND THAT LOOK OVER YOUR FACE

I TOOK MY TIME ON PURPOSE

UNTIL, YOU STARTED SPRAYING THE CAR AGAIN

AND I WAS GETTING SO WET.

I RAN FROM THE CAR AND YOU WET ME UP WITH THE HOSE.

I FINALLY WENT IN THE HOUSE

BLOWING KISSES

I REMEMBER ONE DAY BLOWING KISSES ON YOU

OVER AND OVER, I DID

AND YOU JUST LAUGHED LIKE A LITTLE KID.

AND I SAW YOU AS A CHILD WITH PURE JOY

THE SMILE ON YOUR FACE WAS AN INNOCENT
BOY.

AND

I REMEMBER,

YOU SAID," THANK YOU"

I ASKED YOU WHY

YOU SAID THAT IT REMINDED YOU OF WHAT
YOUR GRANDMA USE TO DO

 AND IT GAVE ME SUCH PLEASURE TO KNOW THAT
I DID THAT FOR YOU

I MADE YOU LAUGH AND GIGGLE

AND REMINDED YOU OF A TIME WHEN YOU WERE
LITTLE.

WHEN ALL WE HAD WAS THAT MOMENT

I REMEMBER THE MOMENT ON THE COUCH

WHEN ALL WE HAD WAS THAT MOMENT

WE SHARED A KISS

AND THEN IT WAS TOO LATE

THE MOMENT HAD BEGUN IN A SECOND

AND BEFORE I KNEW IT THE SECONDS HAD
PASSED

IT WAS BEING A DREAM AND THE DREAM
UNFOLDING RIGHT BEFORE YOUR EYES

BUT YOU'RE IN THE DREAM

ALL WE HAD WAS THAT MOMENT

THERE WAS NO THOUGHT

AND THERE'S WAS NOT ANY EXSPECTATION

JUST FEELING

WHEN ALL THAT WE HAD WAS MOMENT

I COULD TRUST YOU

YOU HELD MY WAIST

AND I COULD TOUCH YOU

AND I WAS SAFE IN YOUR ARMS

AND I COULD BREATH AND TAKE YOU IN

WHEN ALL THAT WE HAD WAS THAT MOMENT

I CLOSE MY EYES AND KNOW THAT YOU WERE
STILL THERE

I COULD FEEL

LIKE THE WIND EVERYWAY

TAKING ME AWAY IN THAT MOMENT

WHEN ALL THAT WE HAD WAS THAT MOMENT

IT WAS US

NOT AGAINST THE WORLD BUT IN A PLACE OF
SERENITY

A PLACE A PEACE

IN AOUR PURIEST FORM

I COULD SEE YOU AND YOU COULD SEE ME

WHEN ALL WE HAD WAS THAT MOMENT

WE SAID NOTHING BUT YET WE WERE TALKING

I HEARD EVERY WORD THAT YOU SAID

IN A MERE THOUGH IN MY HEAD

AND I BELIEVE AND I KNOW THAT YOU HEARD ME
TO

I COULD TELL

BECAUSE EVEY WORD I SPOKE, YOU RESPONDED

WHEN ALL WE HAD WAS THAT MOMENT

PARALYZING KISSES

I SUMMITED MYSELF TO YOU, THE MOMENT I
LOOKED INTO YOUR EYES.

I GAVE A WAY MY CONTROL, THE MOMENT I FELT
YOUR TOUCH.

 I ACCEPTED YOUR KISS

AND WITH THAT KISS, I GAVE OVER MY WILL

I LAIGH TO THINK ABOUT IT,

BECAUSE ALL I COULD DO, WAS BE STILL.

AND ONE KISS TURNED INTO MORE.

YOU KISSED EVERY SPOT WHERE THERE WAS
PAIN.

AND I EMBRACED YOUR KISSES LIKE THEY WERE
MEDICINE.

HEALING ME SOFTLY,

FROM THE PAIN OF OTHERS,

WHOSE TOUCH I COULD NOT FORGET.

YOUR KISSES MADE IT POSSIBLE FOR THE PAIN TO
GO A WAY.

YOU WERE GIVING ME A SHOT WITH EVERY KISS
YOU MADE

AND IT MADE ME PARALYZED FROM HEAD TO MY
FEET.

BARELY CONSCIOUS, I COULD BARELY BREATHE.

I WANTD TO MOVE BUT I WAS PARALYZED

YOUR KISSES WERE GIVING ME LIFE

EVERY KISS, I FELT SO DEEPLY.

THEY WERE LIKE A PARALYTIC DRUG

RENDERING THE MUSCLES OF MY BODY

MAKING IT IMPOSSIBLE FOR ME TO MOVE

BUT TO BE HONEST, I DIDN'T WANT TO.

THE BALLERINA

I HAD A VISION ABOUT A MUSICAL BALLERINA. I REMEMBER SEEING IT TURN AND TURN AROUND.

AND IMMEDIATELY, I KNEW SOMEONE WOULD GIVE IT TO ME

I'D LIKE TO THINK IT WOULD BE MY HUSBAND

I BELIEVED IN THAT MOMENT IT WOULD BE MY HUSBAN.

THEN YOU TOOK ME TO A THRIFT SHOP.

AND RIGHT BEFORE MY EYES WAS THE BALERINA.

I COULDN'T BELIEVE IT.

I WAS SO HOPING YOU WOULD GET IT FOR ME

I KEPT LOOKING BACK TO SEE IF YOU WOULD BUY IT.

BUT I KNEW YOU

AND I THOUGHT,

HE'S NOT GOING TO GET IT.

I ALMOST CRIED WHEN I WALKED AWAY FROM IT

I DIDN'T WANT TO LEAVE IT

WHO WAS GOING TO GET IT?

I REMEMBER THINKING THAT I HAD ENOUGH MONEY FOR IT.

I HAD DECIDED TO GO BACK FOR IT

AND SOMEONE HAD GOTTEN IT

MY HEART SUNK

THEN…...

I THOUGHT IT WAS YOU

HOPED IT WAS YOU

BUT I COULDN'T BELIEVE IT WAS YOU WHO GOT
MY PRECIOUS BALLERINA

A FEW DAYS LATER I WENT INTO YOUR ROOM
AND FOUND CHRISTMAS GIFTS.

I FOUND THE DOLL YOU BROUGHT

AND I LOOKED FOR THE BALLERINA AND TO MY
AMAZEMENT, IT WAS NOT THERE

I HAD GIVEN UP THE NOTION THAT YOU GOT

UNTIL CHRISTMAS DAY

AND I OPENED UP THE BOX AND I SAW MY
BALLERINA

I DIDN'T KNOW WHT TO SAY

I COULDN'T SAY YOU WERE MY HUSBAND

BUT I BELIEVED YOU WERE.

I NEEDED YOU TO TELL ME YOU WERE

BUT THAT BALLERINA WAS MY CONFIRMATION.

THE RAIN POURED DOWN ON US LIKE A SHOWER

THERE WE WERE THE FIRST TIME TOGETHER

STANDING IN THE RAIN

YOU WERE UNSURE

AND IT WAS AKWARD

BUT I TOLD YOU IT WAS OKAY

THERE WAS NOTHING THAT YOU COULD DO
WRONG

BUT LET YOURSELF GO

AND THE WATER BEGAN TO POUR

AND THE RAIN POURED DOWN ON US LIKE A
SHOWER

ON OUR FACE

AND WETTING OUR HAIR

AND YOU GAVE ME KISS,

AS THE WATER CAME DOWN.

BUT WE DIDN'T CARE

THE BEAT OF MY HEART

I HEARD THUNDER

LOUDER THAN ANY BOMB

AND I FOUND MYSELF EMBRACED IN YOUR ARMS.

WE DIDN'T CARE ABOUT THE RAIN.

JUST THE MOMENT THAT WE WERE IN.

I FELT THE TOUCH OF YOUR FACE.

I FELT THE TOUCH OF YOUR SKIN.

AND THE RAIN POURED DOWN ON US LIKE A SHOWER,

COVERING US.

I WAS COLD,

BUT YOU HELD ME CLOSE.

YOU SAW ME AND THERE WAS NOTHING I COULD HIDE.

I SAW YOU FROM THE INSIDE.

AND THE RAIN POURED DOWN ON US LIKE A SHOWER.

ON OUR FACE

AND WETTING OUR HAIR

AND YOU GAVE ME KISS,

YOU AND I WILL ALWAYS BE

YOU'LL ALWAYS BE THE ONE WHO FINDS ME.

I'LL ALWAYS BE THE ONE WHO'S WAITING.

YOU'LL ALWAYS BE THE ONE WHO COVERS ME.

I'LL ALWAYS BE THE ONE UNDER YOU.

YOU'LL ALWAYS BE THE ONE REACHING OUT
YOUR HAND

AND I'LL ALWAYS BE THE ONE HOLDING ON.

YOU'LL ALWAYS BE THE ONE GIVING ME WHAT I
NEED.

I'LL ALWAYS BE THE ONE GIVING YOU WHAT YOU
WANT.

YOU'LL ALWAYS BE THE ONE THAT WILL LISTEN.

I'LL ALWAYS BE THE ONE TO SPEAK.

YOU'LL ALWAYS BE THE ONE WHO LOVES
SILENTLY.

I'LL ALWAYS BE THE ONE TO LOVE OUT LOUD

YOU'LL ALWAYS BE THE ONE

I wanted to express my love in this book

I hope that it inspired someone .

If you liked this book, please try the others below